LEGO STAR WARS®

YODA'S SECRET MISSIONS

LEGO® STAR WARS®

YODA'S SECRET MISSIONS

SCHOLASTIC INC.

"The Phantom Podracer," "Home, Swamp Home," and "Jedi Temple of Doom"
written by Ace Landers.
Illustrated by Ameet Studio

ISBN 978-0-545-65700-6

10 9 8 7 6 5 4 3 2 1   14 15 16 17 18 19/0
Printed in the U.S.A.   40
This edition first Scholastic printing, September 2014

TABLE OF CONTENTS

MAY THE FORCE BE WITH YOU

The Force has always been in the universe. This energy field that surrounds and penetrates everything, the power that binds the galaxy together, is timeless. Ever since its presence was discovered by the seers from the Deep Core world of Tython, the Force has been regarded as a source of both wisdom and power.

The clash between those who—driven by hatred and greed—strove only for power and those who sought peace and enlightenment was inevitable. Soon the devastating Force Wars of Tython broke out. The conflict between the followers of the light side and the followers of the dark side ended with the victory of the light-siders. The end of war marked the beginning of the Jedi Order.

The first Jedi Knights left Tython and spread into the galaxy as the defenders of peace and justice. They settled on Ossus and established a Jedi Academy there. Yet, during the Great Sith War the planet was ravaged and the Jedi found a new home on Coruscant, where they helped to build the peaceful Galactic Republic.

At the helm of the Jedi Order in the last centuries of the Republic stood a powerful Jedi known for his legendary wisdom, mastery of the Force, skills in lightsaber combat, and mischievous sense of humor. A member of a mysterious species, small in size, and very old, he was respected by friends and often underestimated by enemies. His name was Yoda.

THE JEDI TEMPLE

The headquarters of the Jedi Order on Coruscant were established about 5,000 years before the Battle of Yavin. For many centuries, the Jedi Temple was a sanctuary and training facility for the members of the Order and their allies. Many renowned Jedi Knights considered it a great honor to learn the ways of the Force there.

The Republic granted land to the Order hoping the Jedi would build a massive fortress like the one established on Ossus, but the Order chose to build just a small building for meditation that consisted of only several chambers and corridors. However, over the following years functioning in the heart of the peaceful Republic, the Temple grew and a distinctive crown of spires was added to its structure. Soon the Jedi Archives also moved into the Temple along with a modern library.

In the southwest tower of the Temple resided the Jedi High Council. The Council was made up of twelve powerful Jedi Masters who guided the Order and advised the Republic's Supreme Chancellor. Under the leadership of Grand Master Yoda, many promising candidates were given their chance to learn the ways of the Force, many planets were taken under protection, and many secret missions were planned and accomplished in order to keep peace in the galaxy . . .

THE PHANTOM PODRACER

I t was a bleak time for the Jedi Order. Darth Sidious, a powerful Dark Lord of the Sith, was threatening the Galactic Republic, which was at war with the Separatists and their droid armies, led by the evil Count Dooku. Together Sidious and Dooku were building the power of the dark side to overtake the Republic and wipe the Jedi from existence forever. In other words, these were bad guys, and so far they were winning . . . big time.

But one fearless Jedi Master fought on, teaching the secrets of the Force to a new group of Padawans. Yoda was a legendary Jedi, and with the help of his trusty droid sidekicks, C-3PO and R2-D2, he was embarking on one of the

Jedi Temple's training missions . . .

"*Awwww* . . . moisture farms on Tatooine!" grumbled Rako, one of the younglings. "Master Yoda, I hoped this would be a dangerous mission!"

"*Hmmmm,*" said Yoda wisely. "For danger, a Jedi does not look. Danger, a Jedi always finds."

"I, for one, am quite pleased to visit Tatooine," said C-3PO. "Finally, we are taking a responsible field trip to a place where nothing bad ever happens. Oh, we will learn so much about moisture vaporators, nerf herding, and perhaps we can fit in some bantha spotting, too. Plus, it will be bright and sunny this time of year."

"It's always bright and sunny there," said Bobby. "That desert planet has two suns!"

"Wait, don't they have podracing on Tatooine?" asked Vaash Ti. "That would be cool!"

"*Brrrrrrr-shril-we-OWWWW!*" bleeped R2.

"Poor Artoo tried podracing once," explained C-3PO. "*Once.*"

With dashed hopes of any adventure, the Padawans buckled up for one of the most boring rides of their lives. But little did they know that someone else was paying a visit to Tatooine that very same day.

Count Dooku and General Grievous were flying to Tatooine on a special assignment for Darth Sidious.

"Hey, Dooku," said Grievous, "why do people call you Count? I've never seen you count anything."

"Four arms, one heart, and no brain," answered an exasperated Dooku. "Now, pay attention. Darth Sidious is calling in with instructions."

Just then a hologram of Darth Sidious appeared. "Dooku, excellent. I see you've made it to Tatooine. Wait . . . you brought along the cyborg?"

"Hi, Sidious," said Grievous with a goofy smile. "Nice hood. It looks good on you . . . er, I mean, it looks evil on you. Super evil."

"He saw me getting the keys to the ship," interrupted Dooku. "You know how he gets when he thinks you're going

somewhere without him. He just won't stop whining. For a Separatist, he really doesn't like being separated from me."

"Yes, well, perhaps he can be of some use to you on this assignment," said Sidious. "I'm sending you the coordinates now. Believe it or not, even though you'll be on Tatooine, you won't need any sunscreen where you're going."

Not far away, Yoda and the Padawans landed safely next to Mac's Moisture Farm. There was a sign next to the farm that read, LOOKING FOR WATER? WE'VE GOT IT!

C-3PO stepped off the ship first and slathered himself with sunscreen. "One can never be too careful about sun-burns. You look worried, Master Yoda. Would you care for some sun protection, too?"

But Yoda wasn't worried about the sun. He felt a disturbance in the Force. Another ship flew directly overhead. It was a ship that Yoda had seen too many times before. It was Count Dooku! He was here on Tatooine. But why? "Okay, I am," Yoda told Threepio. "Take over the trip, you will. A bigger Jedi to fry, I have."

"Me?!" cried Threepio.

"Him?!" cried the Padawans.

"Oh, my!" said Threepio. "I am a protocol droid, not a tour guide."

"Actually, a perfect moisture farm tour guide, a protocol droid makes, yes?" smiled Yoda.

"Your point, I see," said Threepio.

"Make fun of me, you don't," the Jedi said with a sharp look at the droid. "Talk this way, I have since before you were invented. Now, borrow this landspeeder, I will. On your own, you are!"

"Sorry, Master Yoda," apologized Threepio before gathering the Padawans. "Now, students please follow me if you want to learn every last minutia about water creation, irrigation, and sustainability. I promise we won't waste a drop of your time!"

The farm was quiet except for the pulsating towers that surrounded it. It looked like today had just gone from dull to totally-mind-numbingly-boring. While Threepio struck up a conversation with a moisture vaporator, the Padawans turned to watch Yoda speed away.

"I'll bet he's going somewhere way cooler than here," said Bobby.

"Anywhere is way cooler than here," said Vaash Ti.

No sooner had Yoda left then another vehicle came blazing past the students. It was a podracer, and it was going really fast! The Padawans looked at one another and smiled as it sped by. Just beyond the dunes, there was a billboard they had not seen before. It read, PODRACER RALLY TODAY! ALL RACERS WELCOME.

"Anybody else wanna race?" asked Bene as the Padawans all nodded in agreement. Even R2-D2 whistled to join.

"Wow, the moisture farm is so boring even Artoo couldn't stand it," said Rako.

Quietly, while Threepio was busy with the moisture vaporator, the Padawans scrurried back onto the bus with Artoo and took off for adventure.

At the registration booth, a blue, winged creature named Watto sat holding a sheet of paper. "If you want to race, it'll cost you one hundred truguts," he said.

"We can give you credits," said Vaash Ti with a Jedi mind-trick wave. "Credits will do fine."

"One hundred truguts," said Watto plainly. "And stop waving your hand in my face. What, you think you're some kind of Jedi or something? Mind tricks don't work on me."

"What about a trade, then?" asked Bene. "We'll give you our bus if we lose."

"Sounds good enough to me," agreed Watto.

The Padawans climbed back in their bus and shuttled to the starting line. The crowd roared with laughter seeing the tiny Padawan school bus with its meager engines idling alongside famous podracers. The other podracers looked like wild chariots ready to fly as fast as possible. But the Padawans knew their spaceship had a few tricks up its sleeves.

"Podracers!" shouted the announcer. "Start your engines!" The racecourse echoed with high-pitched gears coming to life. Every podracer let loose a massive hum that shook the stadium. Every podracer except the Padawans'.

"Um, this is a bad time to say this, but my mom says I'm not supposed to podrace," said Bobby.

Then the light turned green and the racers took off, leaving only a cloud of dust behind them. When the smoke settled, the Padawan bus was still waiting at the starting line.

"Okay, I guess we can podrace," said Bobby. The Padawans cheered as Rako flipped a switch, and two giant engines emerged from the back of the bus. With everyone buckled in safely, they blasted off! The bus caught up to the other racers in no time and zipped to the front of the pack.

"First stop, Mos Eisley!" yelled Vaash Ti, holding a map. They darted through the busy streets crowded with ruffians. The checkpoint was straight ahead with a Cantina band playing. The Padawans zoomed around the checkered flag and drowned out the music with roaring engines. But they weren't alone—another racer was fast on their tail! This "phantom podracer" drove a sleek, silver metal ship with dark windows so they couldn't see the driver.

"Next stop, Jabba's Palace!" said Vaash Ti excitedly.

"Look out!" said Rako. "That phantom podracer behind us has some slick moves!" Just as he said this, the silver ship did a 360° curl between two roaming banthas. The Padawans were all impressed, but now wasn't the time to stop and applaud. The ground raced beneath them as they flew across the desert landscape.

"Hey, isn't that Master Yoda?" asked Bobby, pointing to an old landspeeder below them. ZOOM! The bus whizzed past Yoda, who was startled to see the Padawan Bus traveling at

such high speeds, especially when the Padawans should be learning about moisture farms with Threepio. Count Dooku's evil plan would have to wait.

"Do everything, I must," grumbled the Jedi as he used the Force to rebuild his landspeeder into a twin ion engine podracer. The bricks magically rearranged themselves and clicked into place. Then, he was off to help his students.

But the Padawans were going too fast. Yoda tried to catch up, but the mystery podracer blew past, nudging him slightly and sending him off course. The Jedi Master could almost swear he heard the racer apologize. Careening out of control, Yoda crashed right into a Jawa transport. The Jawas were very angry, but Yoda couldn't have landed in a better spot. Using his Force building again, he took spare parts from the Jawas' broken droids to make the biggest, baddest podracer ever!

"*Hmmm*, have head start, they do. Pedal to the metal, I must put," said Yoda as he whooshed back into the race.

The Padawans zipped past Jabba's palace as the Hutt waved to them from his floating barge. But the phantom podracer turned wide and bumped Jabba's barge over, dumping everyone into the sand.

"Watch out for that phantom racer!" said Rako. "He's a wild driver! He's worse than my grandma!"

"Next stop, Dark Side Mining Incorporated!" yelled Vaash Ti. "And step on it!"

As sand whipped around outside, the Padawans could barely make out the last checkpoint. It was nothing but a hole in the ground, but there was another ship parked by

it. Suddenly, as they approached the checkpoint, the phantom podracer slammed into the bus from behind. Veering off course, the bus tumbled down the hole into a maze of mines.

"Great!" cried Rako. "Now we'll never win!"

"Look on the bright side—at least this is a mine shaft and not a Sarlacc," said Bene.

"My mom says I'm not supposed to be eaten by a Sarlacc," said Bobby.

But then, just ahead, the Padawans saw something strange: Count Dooku and General Grievous. Grievous was using his four lightsabers to dig like a drill into the mines and Dooku was talking to a hologram.

"We've almost found it, Lord Sidious!" said Dooku. "A

crystal that will serve as the power source for your new death ray which will be strong enough to destroy an entire planet!"

"What do you think they're doing down here?" Rako whispered, but before anyone had a chance to answer, the Padawan Bus was rammed again by the phantom podracer.

"WHOA!" yelled the Padawans as their bus slammed forward, knocking over Dooku and Grievous and dislodging a giant crystal, which got stuck in the hood of the bus.

"Hey, that crystal belongs to us!" shouted General Grievous.

"Let's get out of here," said Vaash Ti. She punched the gas, and they blasted away. Miraculously, they escaped the mines and were back in the race. The other podracers were just now reaching the last checkpoint. It was going to be a race to the finish line.

The crystal added extra weight, but there was no way to get rid of it now. Zipping in and out of air traffic, the bus made its way to the front of the racers. The Padawans could just see the finish line, when Yoda pulled up next to them.

"Pull over, you will, right now!" he yelled.

The Padawans sighed, but they obeyed the Jedi Master. They

landed their bus and watched the other racers breeze past them to the finish line.

"Sorry, Master Yoda," the Padawans apologized.

"Sorry, you should not be," said Yoda smiling. "Out of the dark side's hands, this deadly crystal, you have kept. Today, the galaxy, you saved."

The Padawans cheered in excitement as Yoda congratulated them, until Watto came over.

"Too bad you didn't win," said Watto. "You had a fifty-to-one shot. Guess I'll be taking my bus now."

"But who is the winner?" asked Bene.

"Some weirdo . . . entered the race after you guys," said Watto. "*Hmmm*, here he is now."

The sleek, silver metal ship landed next to them. The

hatch opened, and the phantom driver walked out. Holding a trophy almost his own size was their substitute teacher!

"Threepio?!" the Padawans exclaimed.

"Of course it's me," said Threepio. "Who were you expecting, a Wookiee? Now, back to the moisture farm everyone. We still have time to see the nerfs . . ."

THE JEDI ORDER

For over a thousand generations the members of the Jedi Order were guardians of peace in the galaxy. They sought solutions to conflicts using logic, tolerance, attentive listening, persuasion, and negotiation. The way of the Jedi was the way of wisdom and patience, backed by swift and resolute action when necessary.

The candidates for Jedi were recruited from beings who were sensitive to the Force. The Order used blood tests to measure their count of midi-chlorians—microscopic life forms that lived in the cells of all living beings. A high midi-chlorian count indicated a being's potential to become a Jedi.

The would-be Jedi learned to use the Force through meditation. Their training required the deepest commitment and most serious mind. Jedi apprentices were encouraged to reject emotions such as passion, fear, anger, and hate. They were not allowed to have strong emotional attachments to others or to material possessions.

The Jedi were bound to a code of virtue, principles and justice. Even though they had formidable combat skills, the Jedi fought only as a last resort. Their way contrasted with their archenemies, the Sith, who used the dark side of the Force to achieve their goal of ruling the galaxy.

YODA'S CHALLENGE

Train themselves the Jedi must, to let go of everything they fear to lose. True or false?

JEDI RANKS

In the last period of the Old Republic, most of the Jedi were instructed by Yoda. It was his guidance that helped them develop their skills as they progressed from the lowest to the highest level of Jedi training.

Jedi Initiate

The youngest members of the Jedi Order. Depending on species, their age varied—for humanoids it could be as young as age two. Those Force-sensitive children were given the rank of Initiate if the Jedi Council decided they were suitable for individual instruction. Initiates were removed from their families and brought to a Jedi academy for formal training.

Jedi Padawan

The rank of Padawan was given to Initiates who completed their training and were chosen by a Jedi Knight or Master for apprenticeship. Padawans were typically taken at adolescence and accompanied their Master everywhere—from simple tasks to dangerous, off-world missions—to learn from experience and personal guidance.

Jedi Knight

After nearly a decade of one-on-one training with a Master, the disciplined Padawans were eligible to attempt the Jedi Trials. If they passed all tests, they became Knights and full members of the Jedi Order. Knights were no longer bound to a Master. They were free to travel the galaxy, accept missions from the Council, or instruct a Padawan.

Jedi Master

The members of the Order who had trained a Padawan to knighthood or demonstrated the deepest understanding of the Force could be promoted by the Jedi Council to the rank of Master. Only Masters were allowed to sit on the Jedi Council. The greatest and wisest of them held the honorific title of Grand Master and was the head of the Order.

THE JEDI CODE

All members of the Jedi Order, from Masters to Padawans, followed a set of general guidelines known as the Jedi Code. In its classic form, written by Master Homonix Rectonia, the Code consists of the following core concepts:

> *There is no emotion, there is peace.*
> *There is no ignorance, there is knowledge.*
> *There is no passion, there is serenity.*
> *There is no death, there is the Force.*

The words of the code encouraged the Jedi to give equal consideration to every being and point of view. To do so, they had to achieve self-discipline and overcome their own needs and urges. The Jedi sought to improve themselves through knowledge and training in order to serve rather than rule, for the good of the galaxy.

YODA'S CHALLENGE

To be ignorant and gain power, is the goal of the Jedi. No consideration to other beings, do they have. True or false?

HOME, SWAMP HOME

As the evil Sith planned their next attack, Master Yoda and Obi-Wan Kenobi left the Jedi Temple on a scouting mission in a Separatist section of space.

"I never knew that space could smell so bad," said Obi-Wan as he pinched his nose inside the spaceship. "It smells like Sarlacc burps after eating a rotten rancor."

"*Hmmm*, nothing bad I smell," said Yoda. "Quite delightful, it smells, yes, *hmmmm*."

Obi-Wan gave the elderly master a crooked look. The stench that surrounded their ship was remarkably stinky.

Perhaps his old friend had lost his sense of smell after years of battling droids until they became heaping piles of scorched metal. "Why are we here anyway? What are we looking for?"

"What we are looking for, I know not," admitted Yoda. "But find it there, we will, on the Bogden moon. Yes, *hmmmmm*."

Shaking his head, Obi-Wan steered the ship down toward the alien planet. The dirty gray clouds parted to reveal swamp as far as the eye could see. Twisted trees weaved in and out of one another like skeleton bones, and under their branches lay a bubbling, gooey marsh. The ship landed on a slimy patch of moss.

Obi-Wan stepped out first and couldn't believe how ugly this planet was. "Who in their right mind would want to live here? Even the Sith aren't that crazy."

But as Yoda stepped off the ship, he squished his feet into the swampy mud and smiled with a contented sigh. "Good on my feet, the sludge feels."

"Well," said Obi-Wan, "can you feel anything else, Master? Besides the mud under your feet?"

"A mild disturbance in the Force, I feel," said Yoda as he focused deeper into the woods. "There."

Obi-Wan armed his lightsaber and put up his guard. "Are enemies close?"

"No." Yoda laughed. "Your weapon, put down. Thinking, I was. A wonderful place for a hut, this would make."

"A what?" asked Obi-Wan.

"A hut," answered Yoda as he wandered over by the woods. "To live in, a home, for me. Yes, *hmmm*."

"If you want to live here, let's at least make sure you'll be all alone," said Obi-Wan as he scoured the area looking for signs of Sith life. "Wait, what are you doing? Where did you find those curtains?"

Yoda smiled and held up two different patterns of cloth against a tree. "What think you, matches the mangrove more— gingham, plaid, or houndstooth, *hmmm*? Or go with drab tan to match my outfit, maybe I should."

Obi-Wan rolled his eyes and worried that his Master may have hit his head on the way to the Bogden moon. "Are you sure you're okay, Master?"

"Better, I've never felt," said Yoda. "A perfect getaway, this will make."

Just then, Obi-Wan heard footsteps sloshing through the swamp. Someone else was there! Immediately the Jedi sprang into action, chasing the footsteps deeper into the gnarled forest. The roots from the trees seemed to reach out

of the ground to try to trip them, but the sure-footed Jedi kept their balance.

As they ran, Obi-Wan could hear Yoda muttering nonsense to himself. "Put a swimming pool here, I could. Heh, heh, heh. Those infinity pools, maybe one of. Cool, that would be."

"Why would you need a pool with all this water around you?" asked Obi-Wan.

"Guests, in case I have. Yes." answered Yoda, pointing. "Over there, an intruder is."

Obi-Wan followed Yoda's gaze and saw another space-ship hidden under a canopy. Next to it, a campfire was burning and beside the fire sat Bossk, one of the Republic's most wanted criminals.

"What's a Trandoshan bounty hunter doing in this neck of the ugly woods?" asked Obi-Wan.

"On vacation in a lovely and relaxing place, clearly he is," said Yoda before stepping out of the forest and into the clearing to address Bossk. "Enjoying Bogden's scenery, are you, *hmmm*?"

Bossk whipped around and drew his gun sending several blasts lashing out at Yoda. The Master Jedi simply diverted each beam. "Great idea, that is," said Yoda. "Make a terrific lighter for campfires, a blaster would." And then he reached out his arm and used the Force to pull the blaster out of Bossk's grip.

Obi-Wan jumped the bounty hunter from behind and captured him. "What are you doing here?"

"Picking up stolen goods for Jabba the Hutt," said Bossk angrily. "This dump of a planet was supposed to be deserted, so I've been using it as a hideout for our goods."

"Yoda, you're a genius," said Obi-Wan. "And here I was thinking that you really did love this place and wanted to move here so badly that you left the Jedi Temple unattended just for a bizarre house hunting mission. I apologize for having the wrong idea. Clearly, you were just here to disrupt a smuggler's trade route."

"Yes, my idea all along, that was, heh, heh, heh," said Yoda nervously as he folded up the blueprints for his secret hut. "Almost had you, I did, *hmmm*? Very silly idea right now, building a secret home on a hidden planet, would be. Forget I mentioned it. Sure everything will turn out fine with the Republic, I am. Heh, heh, heh."

Maybe find a less crowded swamp planet, I will, Yoda thought to himself.

LIGHTSABER

The Jedi's weapon of choice was the lightsaber. Not as crude and loud as a blaster, the lightsaber was an elegant weapon and a symbol of the righteous protectors of the galactic peace. To carry a lightsaber indicated incredible skill, dexterity, and attunement to the Force.

The earliest clashes between the light and the dark side were fought with metal blade swords Force-enhanced for strength and sharpness. For millennia, the Jedi sought out a superior weapon that would enable them to fully utilize their skills in using the Force. Finally, the combination of advanced offworld technology with experiments on how to "freeze" a laser beam, resulted in creating the first lightsaber.

Every lightsaber consisted of a metal hilt that emitted a blade of pure plasma. The hilt contained all the weapon's mechanisms, including a power cell and a set of crystals that focused the plasma beam. The lengths of the hilt and the blade varied greatly as the Jedi constructed their individual weapons themselves to suit their own specific needs.

The lighsaber could deflect blaster bolts and cut through almost anything. Only a few materials found in the galaxy could withstand its blow, for instance Mandalorian iron called *beskar* or a rare metal known as *cortosis*. The Zillo Beast from Malastare had skin resistant to lightsaber blows, too.

Among many variants of the lighsaber were: training lightsabers with a permanent low-power setting for limited injury used by Jedi younglings, or double-bladed light-sabers originally invented by the Sith. There were even lightwhips and special lightsabers to use underwater.

Lightsabers were an important part of the Knighting ceremony of the Jedi Order. During the ceremony, the would-be Knight knelt before the Master who lowered the lightsaber blade to his or her shoulder and cut off the Padawan braid in a swift motion. The event was witnessed by the members of the Council holding up their ignited lightsabers.

YODA'S CHALLENGE

The mark of a Jedi or . . . Sith, the lightsaber is. Its wielder's good or bad intentions, the lightsaber blade's color reflects.
True or false?

SIZE MATTERS **NOT**

Standing about sixty-six centimeters tall, Yoda was considered to be one of the greatest swordsmen of all time. It was said that only Mace Windu and Count Dooku were able to fight with him on equal terms.

There were seven forms of lightsaber combat and Yoda mastered them all, but Form IV called *Ataru* was his favorite, because it allowed him to overcome the limitations of his height and reach. His combat style heavily relied on jumps and acrobatic moves. Despite his age, Yoda showed amazing speed and dexterity, leaping through the air and twirling as he dodged the opponent's blows and counterattacked in a split second with his green-bladed lightsaber.

Yoda was also one of the most skilled users of the Force in the history of the galaxy. His legendary ability to telekinetically move enormous objects or to disarm an opponent with a gentle gesture of his small hands or to see the future through the Force made him the most respected Jedi of his era. As the head of the Jedi Council, Yoda was involved in politics and solving conflicts, but at heart, he was a teacher who strongly believed in the importance of passing knowledge to younger generations.

YODA'S CHALLENGE

Nothing wrong there is, with trying the ways of the dark side. Change your mind, always possible it is. True or false?

JEDI TEMPLE OF DOOM

It was a normal morning at the Jedi Temple. The Padawans were preparing for their class, waiting for Master Yoda to arrive. Instead, C-3PO entered the room and made an announcement.

"Class, I have some good news, some bad news, and some great news. The bad news is that Master Yoda has been called away. The good news is that I will be your substitute teacher for today. The great news is that we have a new student!"

A young boy with dark hair stood next to Threepio. He smiled innocently and waved to the class.

"Younglings, please give a warm, Jedi welcome to Bob, our newest Padawan," said Threepio. "Bob, why don't you tell us a bit about yourself?"

"Um, my name is Bob A. Fett," said the new student, "and I, um, was home-schooled before, but now I'm, uh, like, super psyched to learn the ways of the Force and stuff."

All the Padawans shook hands with the new student— except for Bobby. He didn't trust the new kid. There was something about him that seemed—wrong. Plus, he didn't like another student having such a similar name.

"It's very exciting to have a new face in the class- room, Bob," said Threepio. "So let's get ready to learn a few lessons." Threepio studied Yoda's notebook. "It looks like Master Yoda planned for some lightsaber practice first."

Instantly, training droids flew into the room. The Padawans jumped up, grabbed their training lightsabers, and put on their blast shield hel- mets, except for Bob. He watched as the train- ing droids shot energy shocks at the Padawans who couldn't see where the blasts were coming from. They were using the Force to block the attacks with their lightsabers!

"Do you have a training lightsaber, Bob?" asked Threepio as he handed the new student a blast shield helmet.

"Oh, uh . . . yeah, I do." Bob smiled. With one smooth move, Bob put on his helmet and powered up a giant lightsaber. As his training droid swooped down, Bob rolled over to avoid its first attack and slashed the droid in half with one swipe. Then he twirled around the rest of the room attacking the other training droids, narrowly missing the Padawans with each strike. Soon the entire training floor was covered with broken, electronic guts.

The Padawans raised their blast shields in wonder of what just happened. "Are you sure that's a training lightsaber?" asked Rako.

"Oh, dear!" cried Threepio. "It seems you are a little too eager to prove yourself, Bob. In this classroom we use training droids to hone our skills. How will you ever learn to better your reaction times or your attack accuracy if you treat these droids like piñatas?"

"*Hmmm*, I'd say his reaction time and accuracy are already honed," said Vaash Ti with a smile.

"I don't trust him," Bobby muttered under his breath.

"I'm sorry," apologized the new youngling nervously. "This is the way I've trained in the past. I'll be more careful next time."

"That was so cool!" exclaimed some of the Padawans. "How did you do that?"

"I don't know," admitted Bob. "Lots of practice, I guess."

"Yes, well, ahem," Threepio cleared his throat to get the students' attention. "Padawans, let's clean up this mess."

With one giant Force push, the Padawans swept the floor clean and lifted the droid debris into a box.

"Okay, now we are going to—" Threepio paused to read over Yoda's teaching notes for the day, "Oh, goodness. According to Yoda, every Jedi must be prepared for even the most extreme form of combat. Your next exercise will be, *gulp*, hand-to-hand combat. Bring in the clones!"

A group of clone troopers marched into the room in an orderly fashion. While the Padawans and clones paired up as sparring partners, Threepio gave them all a gentle reminder. "Remember, this is only a training session. Padawans, please focus on your defensive skills. Clones, please remember that you are practicing with younglings, not Separatists, so be mindful not to hurt anyone."

Bob shook hands with his clone partner. "Hey, I'm Bob. I'm new here, so take it a little easy on me, okay?"

"*Hmmm*, if you're new here, then why do you look so familiar?" the clone asked.

"I guess I just have one of those faces." Bob smiled. "Should we fight now?"

The trooper lunged at Bob without warning, but the new student shifted to the side and pushed the clone down on the ground. The clone's second attack was faster as he tried to grab Bob by the shoulders, but Bob dropped under him, grabbed the clone's arms, and pulled them between the

clone's legs, which flipped the trooper into the air. He landed on his back with a thud as Bob skidded to safety. Then the new student whipped out a rope and lassoed the clone's arms and legs together.

"Done!" Bob squealed with joy. "How'd I do?"

The other Padawans and clones had all stopped their training to watch Bob work. They were stunned at his speed and skill.

"Well done," marveled Threepio. "I can see Yoda will have his hands full with you, Master Fett."

As the troopers removed their very hog-tied (and very embarrassed) clone companion, the Padawans surrounded Bob with cheers. But Bobby hung back. He had a bad feeling about this new, mysterious student who was suddenly super good at everything. Bobby couldn't figure out why he felt this

way, but Yoda taught him to trust his instincts. And something in his gut warned him to keep a close eye on Bob A. Fett.

During lunch, Bobby watched Bob sneak away from the group. He followed Fett as the new student wandered around the Jedi Temple. Fett peeked into room after room as if he were looking for something. "I knew it!" Bobby whispered quietly to himself. "What is he up to?"

Finally, Fett found what he was looking for: the Jedi Archives. Bobby snuck in after him, keeping a safe distance so as to remain hidden. He watched as Fett quickly searched through the archives. Then Fett pulled out a small glowing crystal.

"Here you are," Fett said with a satisfied look on his face. "Someone will pay a pretty penny for you!"

"The Kyber Crystal!" shouted Bobby. "That memory crystal has a list of all Force-sensitive children in the entire galaxy! You can't take that!"

"Yes, I can!" called out Fett. He darted past Bobby, pushing down a pile of holocrons to block the exit.

"Help!" screamed Bobby. "Bob A. Fett is stealing the Kyber Crystal!"

The Padawans felt Bobby's warning and jumped into action. They quickly cornered the new student, but Fett blasted through a wall with his jetpack. The Padawans trailed him into the clone training area, but they couldn't find Fett anywhere.

"Who is this kid?!" asked Rako. "I want a jet pack so I can fly!"

"Where did he go?" Bobby said. "We have to find him!"

"Tell you where and who he is, I will," said Yoda as he burst into the room. " A new student, Bob A. Fett is not. Boba Fett, he is. Jango Fett's unaltered clone."

"How do we find him?" asked Vaash Ti looking over the room filled with masked clones.

"Like this!" called out Yoda, using the Force to lift the smallest clone into the air. "A bit small for a clone trooper, you are. Bobby's warning, I felt. Come to help, I did."

Boba struggled at first, but then had an idea. "Hey, look, it's Darth Sidious!" he screamed and pointed behind Yoda.

"Sidious! Here?!" yelled Yoda as he whipped around to find Chancellor Palpatine in the hallway.

"Huh?" asked Palpatine nervously. "It's just me. Good old Palpatine. No Darth Sidious here."

"It's a trick . . . *er*, trap, I mean!" said Yoda as Boba Fett shot a grappling hook and pulled free of the Force hold. He scurried away with the Padawans and Yoda hot on his trail.

As he darted around the corners, looking for any way out, Boba found an emergency exit that led through the droid medical center. All around Boba, parts and pieces of droids hung on the wall. The smashed training droids from earlier were being rebuilt and instantly recognized him.

Boba ran back out of the exit, chased by an angry army of hovering training droids zapping him with stun blasts.

Yoda and the Padawans stopped to watch the droids have their revenge. "Something you don't see every day, this is," remarked Yoda before joining in the chase again. "Save the Kyber Crystal, we must!"

As Boba raced outside to his spaceship, he held tight to the Kyber Crystal in his hand. "I got what I came for!" he called out to Yoda and the Padawans. "Na-nanny-boo-boo, I'm gonna destroy you!"

But as he taunted the Jedi with the crystal, he felt a tug and the crystal flew out of his hand.

"My mother says I'm not supposed to play with bounty hunters," Bobby said as he used the Force to recapture the Kyber Crystal. The lone Padawan had been waiting to ambush Fett by his spaceship!

With no other options, Boba Fett jumped into his ship and made an escape without the crystal.

"Wait!" called out Threepio as he joined the crew. "Bob left without his grade report. In my opinion, he was a wonderful student."

"*Hmmm*, much to learn, you have, Threepio," said Yoda as the Padawans all laughed and shook their heads.

JEDI QUIZ

Long is the history of the Jedi Order, and there are still many amazing facts worth knowing. But now let's see what you have learned from this book. Read the questions and mark the correct answer to each of them.

1. What was the role of the Jedi Knights in the galaxy?
   a) They explored unknown worlds.
   b) They guarded peace and justice.
   c) They fabricated lightsabers for sale.

2. What planet were the Jedi Order's headquarters located on?
   a) Tatooine
   b) Yavin
   c) Coruscant

3. Who were the Force-using archenemies of the Jedi?
   a) The Sith Lords
   b) The Jawas
   c) The Hutts

4. What did the Jedi use to discover a Force-sensitive being?
   a) Personality tests
   b) Blood tests
   c) A Jedi detector

5. What's the rank of a Jedi Knight's individual apprentice?
   a) Initiate
   b) Padawan
   c) General

6. What was the typical weapon of the Jedi?
   a) Blaster
   b) Smile
   c) Lightsaber

7. How many Jedi Masters sat in the Jedi Council?
   a) 8
   b) 10
   c) 12

8. What materials are resistant to a lightsaber blade?
   a) There are no such materials.
   b) Only other lightsaber blades.
   c) Beskar and cortosis.

9. What was Form IV of the lightsaber combat called?
   a) Ataru
   b) Ossus
   c) Watto

10. How tall was Grand Jedi Master Yoda?
    a) About eighty centimeters
    b) About sixty centimeters
    c) About forty centimeters

ANSWERS

Page 27
The Jedi Order

True. The Jedi could not be hindered by fear of losing anyone or anything that was close to their heart. Master Yoda used to teach that fear led to anger, anger led to hate, and hate led to suffering . . . Fear was the path to the dark side.

Page 31
The Jedi Code

False. The Jedi respected all life, in any form. They used their extraordinary powers to defend and protect the other, weaker beings. The true Jedi never thought of themselves but sacrificed their lives to public service, law, and peace-keeping.

Page 41
Lightsaber

False. The color of a lightsaber's blade depended on the kind of focusing crystals that were used for its construction. The Jedi chose natural crystals of many different colors. The Sith traditionally used synthetic, red crystals infused with dark energy.

Page 43
Size Matters Not

False. "Once you start down the dark path, forever will it dominate your destiny; consume you, it will," said Yoda many times to his students.

Pages 60-61
Jedi Quiz

1–b, 2–c, 3–a, 4–b, 5–b, 6–c, 7–c, 8–c, 9–a, 10–b.

DISCOVER MORE
LEGO® STAR WARS™
BOOKS!